BEACH VOICES

BEACH VOICES

IF THEY HAD A VOICE

BRAD AYERS

Night Rain Books

Cover Illustration by Allyson Durkin

FIRST EDITION

Printed in the United States of America

ISBN 978-17348739-9-3

Night Rain Books / Night Rain Press
PO Box 445
Tillamook, OR 97141

Night.Rain.Press@gmail.com
http://NightRainBooks.com

CONTENTS

INTRODUCTION TO BEACH VOICES

The beach is a wonderful place we always approach with anticipation and memories that go far back, even to our childhood.

It revives all our senses and gets them going faster and faster as we approach.

We hear it first.

The faint and then growing surf, rolling and crashing on the sand.

Then that unmistakable salt air smell. We know it for certain like we had never left.

The sudden increase in the breeze on our face only briefly slows our approach.

And finally, we feel the sand between our toes getting everywhere to say—hello again.

Are you ready to hear what the Beach Voices have to say?

1

THE HOPEFUL BEACH ROCK

Oh—hello there! Go ahead and
pick me up.

I must have caught your eye. Was
it my shape or color, texture or
size?

Now that you hold me—not so
fast please.

I really deserve your complete attention just for a minute.

After all, I have been waiting here for many decades, too many
to count, actually.

I feel special for once. And yes, there are many beach rocks to
choose from, and you can only carry a few. I know I am not one
of those heart-shaped rocks you see people googling over, or the
ones they call agates you can see light through or even those
red, green or brown jaspers, jades, and even fossils and shells.
But I am special in other ways from all these others. I have even
gotten smoother and rounder from my years rolling in the sea,

with sand and rocks. And, by the way, even lost a little weight the last thousand years or so. I really get tired just lying around with all these other rocks. Even the driftwood gets boring.

I hope I am one who gets to go home with you.

But what is your home like? Will I end up in a coffee table display with other rocks that have caught your eye? I hope I mean more to you. I hope I am the most special beach rock of all.

Oh—looks like we are going to walk a bit. I would rather be in your pocket by now rather than carried loosely in your hand. Tell me you are not just waiting until a better choice comes along. That would be so cruel. Other friends of mine have told similar stories and it did not end well with them. They not only were replaced but thrown down hard, and in one case tossed way over a sand dune where there were no other rock friends. Who knows if they will ever get another chance?

Oh no, are you stopping and bending down? Boy, that was close, just a quick look at a broken sand dollar this time.

But the looking isn't over, is it?

I now realize my competition is almost any other thing that catches your eye.

My odds of going home in your pocket are rather slim.

2

SEAGULL THINKING

 WHAT A LOVELY DAY TO BE A seagull. I see you walking below.

Since you are reading this, I take it you are not one of us.

Well, too bad, because we get to soar on the sea breeze with little or no effort. Great gas mileage requiring just a few sea scraps to fuel the feathers so to speak.

I just got back from my noon job at the McDonalds parking lot. You see, we seagulls are just like humans looking for the fast food lunch. On a good day you might catch a discarded hamburger remnant, or chicken nugget in the parking lot. Bad days, which there seem to be more of, you are lucky to get tossed a French fry. And even then, you have to hustle and grab, then scurry away to defend your catch. And this is after working the lot, car after car, even giving the surprise "car hood landing" a try to shake one free. But more often these days, rather than a tossed token fry to get you to leave, you get the rude windshield wiper brush-off.

Ah, but now I am back on the coast where competition is based on speed and opportunity, not bluffing and intimidation. Yes, there are more birds than just seagulls with all kinds of different skills. Some dive, some soar, and others stand silent for their meal opportunity. I just glide low along the beach and can spot a tasty morsel and make a quick landing. I squawk a lot, almost any time, and for any reason, and I know you can't figure out why. Just because I can't whistle and chirp like those little birds you say I can't sing. Who knows if my squawking, as you call it, isn't a seagull's most beautiful seagull singing?

So much you don't know about me, or me about you. We share the same sand and water with different purposes.

Sad that we may never meet to find out.

3

DRIFTWOOD RESTING

Once a stately sentential, tall, green branched, and reaching to the sky. Yes, I was quite something those many years ago.

Now a lonely driftwood log, no bark left, lying down, and silent.

I see you come and go every day. Some of you stop to sit a while and share your silent thoughts. When there are more of you, I hear voices, laughter at times, and sometimes angry words mostly brief and then resolved. Children are the most fun when they try to walk my trunk or build a shelter just for them. I feel best at these times because I am useful again. Who knew after my fall and the water washed me out to sea that I could again give something of myself? I guess I should give some credit to the water, sand, and rocks who have smoothed me so you could sit so comfortably. I also get a lot of pictures taken, especially of my lower parts where my roots started. Tangled and twisted, but strong and resolved, they get special attention. But enough of my doting and the history lesson.

Let's talk about you. Why do you come to visit? You seem to just wander around, pausing, picking up shells, rocks, and even small driftwood pieces that once belonged to big trees like me. Sometimes younger ones run and chase after their dogs. But you seem to have no purpose or urgency. Is that your normal state? What a wonderful thought if it were true. But I suspect, since you always leave, you are briefly just escaping some other reality. I hope your brief stay has put some charge in your batteries and renewed your life purpose.

The next time you come you may not find me here. I tend to move around the coast on high tides and storms. You see I am now a lonely traveler with not too much to say where I go. Not like the old days where my roots ran deep and wide, securing my stand against wind and rain.

But don't worry. I will probably find another beach to rest on and perhaps give someone like you the chance to sit and wonder the "who and why" just like you have been wondering about today.

4

SANDCASTLES

Hey—watch where you are going with me.

I'm just a grain of sand and there are plenty of us to build any castle you want.

Yes, we all work together and with just the right amount of sea water you can really form some amazing shapes with walls, towers, and tunnels. Oh yes, almost forgot—we need your imagination, little hands and fingers, sand shovels, and if you must, a few driftwood sticks. But not being too boastful, we sand grains are the most important part no matter what else you add.

You work merrily along with your parents watching and advising your construction. Based on how you push us around I think you take us sand grains for granted. We are much more special than you ever could think. You obviously have had no sand grain history lessons.

You know what really gripes us? The emotional indulgence people give to snowflakes. They say they are so beautiful and that no two are exactly the same. Well let's just say there are a lot of different designs and no two have been found to be the same —yet. The same can be said about us, so give us some credit. No one has found two of us alike and up close we are quite unusual.

Another thing—snowflakes only last a few seconds and then they melt so you can't make anything out of them. This is where we stand out. Sand grains have been around for all time, almost. And we will be here for your sandcastles every time you come to visit.

One last thing. How many snowflakes are there compared to us grains of sand? Oh—so many questions you have your lifetime to try and answer.

You are almost finished and then disaster strikes. The tide is rising and down comes your wonderful sand creation. It makes you sad and mad. You rush to try diversions of trenches and mounds to delay the inevitable. But in the end, you must accept the fate that befalls all sandcastles. That was why you saw none made by the kids yesterday when you arrived this morning.

"Time to go," your parents call out.

So, you pack up and abandon what is left of your sandcastle. Will you build another, bigger, stronger, and more beautiful, or move on in life with just the memories?

5

WAVE DREAMER

HERE I COME.

I see you watching.

Let me again, over and over, give you peace and comfort. Neither of us can explain it exactly. Why do I keep returning, and why you keep watching? I suppose there are as many reasons as anything else we can think of. We both must need each other. I try my best to be the perfect wave and make change after change to keep you interested. You keep watching and hoping to see some magic clue as to why and how I do it. Neither of us has the answer but we keep trying.

I suppose my biggest benefit for you is taking your mind to faraway places. Places you can never go without my help. I can put you almost into a spiritual dream-like state. You can go anywhere and think any thoughts you want. Sometimes you stay for hours. You never want to leave and reluctantly move slowly away, often casting one or more last looks.

And when you return, as you most always do, you start the mood shift all over again. It's like you never left even if we have been apart years. We are again partners. You want to call me your own and start searching for the very wave we had last time you were here. I try my best to please you but, like you, I have moved on just a bit due to circumstances not always in my control. But after a few minutes we soon find that comfort zone and start moving off to faraway places in mind and spirit. Again, I am taking you to places you can't go yourself. What a wonderland we often find, if just for a few moments in time.

Before you leave this time, there is another thing I should tell you about. Actually, it involves you and a friend. Yes, I often work the same mood trance we have been discussing when you bring someone you want to talk to. Someone you really care about. I am not jealous you do this as I now become part of something you and your friend cannot do alone. I give you the indescribable feeling of letting go just a bit. You can dig deeper into long protected emotions than you ever could before. You even feel comfortable sharing them.

Us three, the wave, together we are now bonded.

Time to go, but one last look until next time.

6

SEA BREEZE MAGIC

LET'ER GO, RUN, PULL, LET IT OUT, see it raise, up, up, so high.

Then a surprise dive, down, down to the sand. Everything OK? Start over.

Welcome to the beach. My breeze and the sand make kite flying the best. I can hear you yelling.

Well, I see you have finally got that kite thing of yours up in my breeze and in the air. I will keep blowing most of the day so have a good time. I warn you however, you better keep a close watch out. I am known for sudden shifts, lulls, and bursts. I can catch even the most experienced kite flyers by surprise.

But now I see you have some older help. Is that your dad? I bet he has done this before but perhaps quite a long time ago. He looks like he is being a kid again. Running, laughing, jumping. Good for you and him to have this special day together.

Remember how it makes you feel when you get the chance again years from now. You can give back something special.

New kite technology has added some fun shapes, flying tricks, and stability, so this may be new to your dad after all. He will be learning just like you. I think he forgot a few things. But that's the fun of it. New and renewed discovery of something almost magical.

How can that dragon shape fly? Look at those sharks, birds, butterflies, and even octopus with long tentacles for a tail. And look over there, a fish, and a cartoon, and more and more. All such vivid colors. It seems this is going to be a great kite flying day. And look, everyone having such fun.

Let out as much string as you can to see it go higher. Test its limits and your skill. Now, don't take me for granted. I usually get stronger in the afternoon—sometimes too strong for your kite, and we don't want anything to spoil the day. So perhaps you need to start winding in your kite. It's been quite a wonderful day with you and your dad. I bet you will remember this day as one of your special days with him. Keep it in your special memory file ready for occasional recall when life gets challenging.

I promise to be here if you return.

I know you will.

Bring a little friend.

7

TOES IN AN ENDLESS OCEAN

COLD AT FIRST. THEN WE GET TO know each other.

I keep moving and so do you. I have this endless energy. You just want to keep warm. I always get the same reaction—a lot of jumping and splashing as you enter for the first time. And some yelling too.

Come on, a little further out where my waves are. Be careful, but don't be afraid. You are sensing my power as I move in and then out. I can almost pull and push you off your feet. You sense the sand and water running around your toes and it feels good. You seem to be enjoying your visit. And now after a few minutes you are proud of your accomplishment and wave back to your shore friends to come on in. They wave back but remain on the sand.

Oh well, they are not you. You are the risk taker. The adventurer. So am I. I have been around the globe in many oceans and touched many feet just like yours. I hear different voices but the highs and lows they shout all tell the same excited story of doing something a little dangerous and risky. And you feel stronger and perhaps more worldly. You will remember it and re-tell about this day over and over. The day you braved the mighty Pacific.

Could it be some of my travels are rubbing off on you? Distant shores and far-away places. You seem to have forgotten all the day's frustrations as you dance and play in my surf. Really good feeling isn't it? Watch out! Sorry, I guess you didn't see that wave coming. I am full of them so get ready for the next one. Don't struggle against it. Let it take you in its embrace and feel the exhilaration for a moment. I will soon calm and give you a chance to regain your senses.

I see you are nearing the end of your swim in my water. A move back to shore usually means no return in these Northwest waters. Too cold for most to try a second dip. As you dry off and your teeth stop chattering, you look back to me with that respectful parting thanks. It's been amazing, you say—not out loud, but I heard you so clear.

It means just as much.

AFTERWORD: IF THEY HAD A VOICE

Have you ever wondered what our world has to say?

We go about our lives midst all forms of non-human objects with only a passing thought, or no thought at all about them. And rarely have we even attempted a conversation.

What if we listen closely? What would they tell us? What could we learn?

You might be surprised at just how much they have to say about us.

This series of short stories started by an impromptu response to a prompt given in a writing class I took. The prompt was to write for 14 minutes on "something you keep." Out of the blue the image of a beach rock in my hand came to mind. Probably from one of many walks on the beach at Cape Meares, and even seeing others looking for that special rock. Or even seeing some-one's beach and shell collection neatly arranged or scattered around. We all have picked up a beach rock, held it a while, and maybe kept it to go home or dropped it for another. That day I wrote about this experience, completed the assignment, and filed it away with that hint of something undone.

Several months later as I was typing my handwritten responses to past writing prompts into the computer, I again read the story I had titled, "The Hopeful Beach Rock." I lingered a while, reading it again several times. And for some mysterious reason the stories started coming one after the other about other beach objects like driftwood, waves, the ocean breeze, and more. All had something to say about us. They even ask questions and heard our thoughts. They started our memories working and recalling earlier times, ones that were happy, sad, and adventurous.

After doing several beach stories I started to get images of other things we pass by, touch, or work with that should also get a chance to talk. Thus, started a much larger series of stories including things we sit on, doors we go through, and a range of others you will want to read about in the Voices collections.

This is the best part. I realized that in telling these as short stories, some call flash fiction, I could give you the chance to make it your own. I give each a range of emotions and experiences, but you will find it compelling to fill in and expand with your own.

As you read the stories remember only the non-human object does the talking. You have only to listen. The chair, for example, will ask you to remember what you were doing and thinking as you sat for a while, then suggests answers and asks even more questions. The door will recall memories of your emotions the door had observed as you passed through. Like a mirror, the door reflects these and suggests what you were thinking and whether you had any regrets. The beach rock wonders and asks you if you will keep it or discard it and choose another leaving you to determine the outcome. Interesting life lessons for sure.

Each reader of these stories will have a unique reaction to the observations and answers to the questions because all have different experiences. The one common link is we all have these kinds of memories. And each subsequent reading will only add to the recall and variations, with even new themes and outcomes of your own.

Some stories were written on the lighter side of things, playful, and happy times. Some are more serious with only hints of deeper concerns, but none are scary or tragic. Some have a moral bent and others suggest you read between the lines to get the nuance.

Most stories, however, are just plain fun.

ABOUT THE AUTHOR

I give most of the inspiration credit to the wonderful Northwest and Oregon coast. I arrived in 2015 and have not stopped creating in new and unusual ways. It inspires all art forms, and frankly just about anything you want to do. So, I give thanks for a second chance to prosper including my efforts of fiction writing and just recently song writing.

After a first degree in Fine Arts from California State University I went into business for my professional life. An MBA from the University of Denver followed while working for three major US companies, then running and starting my own along the way.

Concurrent to the business side I was an adjunct professor in the MBA program for the University of Phoenix for over 30 years.

I guess I was destined to return to the creative side of life, now at the ripe old age of 81. Old dogs, new tricks? Perhaps in this case. Yes, this is not your typical "about the author?" Blame the weather.

VOICES PUBLICATION COLLECTION

Beach Voices

Doors We Walk Through

The Chair Has Something To Say

Walk In My Garden

What's In The Box

Clothes Get Testy

Food Talks Back

ALSO BY BRAD AYERS

A Life's Journey

www.ingramcontent.com/pod-product-compliance
Lightning Source LLC
Chambersburg PA
CBHW020323150626
46552CB00022B/3180